GOLDIE'S NAP

NICOLE RUBEL

HarperCollins*Publishers*

Goldie's Nap
Copyright © 1991 by Nicole Rubel
Printed in the U.S.A. All rights reserved.
1 2 3 4 5 6 7 8 9 10
First Edition

Library of Congress Cataloging-in-Publication Data
Rubel, Nicole.
    Goldie's nap / Nicole Rubel.
        p.   cm.
    Summary: Mischievous Goldie doesn't want to take a nap at
her day care center.
    ISBN 0-06-025106-9. — ISBN 0-06-025107-7 (lib. bdg.)
    [1. Naps (Sleep)—Fiction.   2. Sleep—Fiction.   3. Day care
centers—Fiction.]   I. Title.
PZ7.R828Gp 1991   90-4401
[E]—dc20   CIP
                                              AC

To my husband Richard

SCISSORS   PAINTS   CHALK

YARN   CRAYONS   PASTE

BABY   ABC

BLOCKS

Mr. Webb read a story to his class.

"Everyone lie down and go to sleep," said Mr. Webb.

"It's nap time," announced Mr. Webb.

"Naps are for babies," said Goldie.

"Time for your nap, Goldie," said Mr. Webb.

"Naps are for babies," said Goldie.

"It's *nap time*," said Mr. Webb.

Goldie tossed and turned. She kicked her neighbor, Carla.

"Go to sleep, Goldie," oinked Carla.

Goldie whistled the class song.

"Shhh . . . ," whispered Pete.

"Naps are for babies," said Goldie. She crawled under her mat.

"There are just a few more minutes of naptime, Goldie," said Mr. Webb.

Goldie watched a caterpillar.

She climbed up after it.

"A flying garbage can!" cried Pete.

"Goldie!" said Mr. Webb.

"This is how you take a nap," said Mr. Webb.

"Naps are for babies," said Goldie.

"Snack time," said Mr. Webb.

"Milk and cookies!" yelled Goldie.

"And now it's time to play," said Mr. Webb.

But Goldie didn't hear him.

She was fast asleep.